Something About Grandma

Tania de Regil

CANDLEWICK PRESS

One early morning in July, Grandma arrived from a long way away with a suitcase in hand. She was there to take Julia for their first summer together without Mom and Dad.

Grandma lived outside of Mexico City, in a town cuddled against a great mountain. At the foot of the mountain was a cobblestone street lined with ash trees. And at the end of the street, a pink bougainvillea crawled over a little old house: Grandma's house.

The back door of the house led to a shrubby garden where Grandma grew lavender, jasmine, daisies, pink geraniums, and purple orchids; lime, plum, and orange trees; and a great big jacaranda tree.

At Grandma's, everything seemed different, and everything was new to Julia.

In the morning, Grandma bought sweet, sugary bread from a woman who carried it in a basket on top of her head.

And in the afternoon, Grandma picked herbs from the garden,
and stirred them into one big pot that simmered and steamed.

There was something about this place, Julia thought, where the sunset skies were filled with birdsong, and the warm breeze was sweet like jasmine. And there was definitely something about Grandma, too.

Grandma seemed to know everything.
Like when Julia snuck into the garden
to pick daisies and limes.

Grandma could also see into the future. She could always tell if Julia was about to fall when she went too fast on her bike.

And Grandma had many secrets. Every night,
she sat quietly in the garden terrace, and wrote
things in a notebook by the light of the moon
and the stars.

One day, a letter from Mom and Dad
arrived, and that's when Julia realized
how much she missed her home.

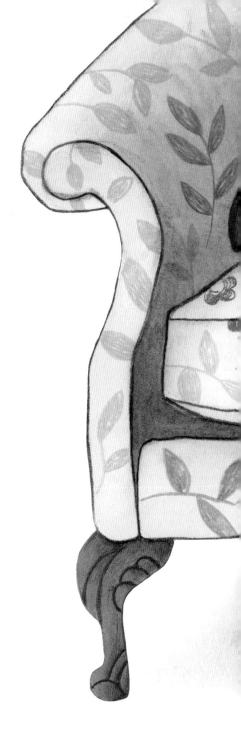

Luckily, Grandma knew just what to do.

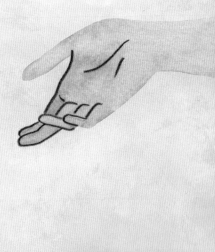

Grandma, it turned out, could fit
Julia perfectly into her arms and
make her feel warm all around.

Grandma could also brew up the most magnificent
hot chocolate at any given time.

Grandma knew all the best tricks . . .

and games.

And she even shared her greatest secret—how to journey back in time.

One morning, when Grandma and Julia were in the garden, the back door creaked open behind them. Julia looked up and there they were. Mom and Dad!

But someone new had come along;
he was small, and he was crying.

Luckily, Julia knew just
what to do.

"Thank you," said Mom.
"It's exactly what we needed.
How did you know?" Julia
looked at Grandma and
smiled.

There was something about this place, Julia thought, where the night was filled with the grasshopper's music, and the warm breeze whistled through the trees. And there was definitely something about Grandma, too.

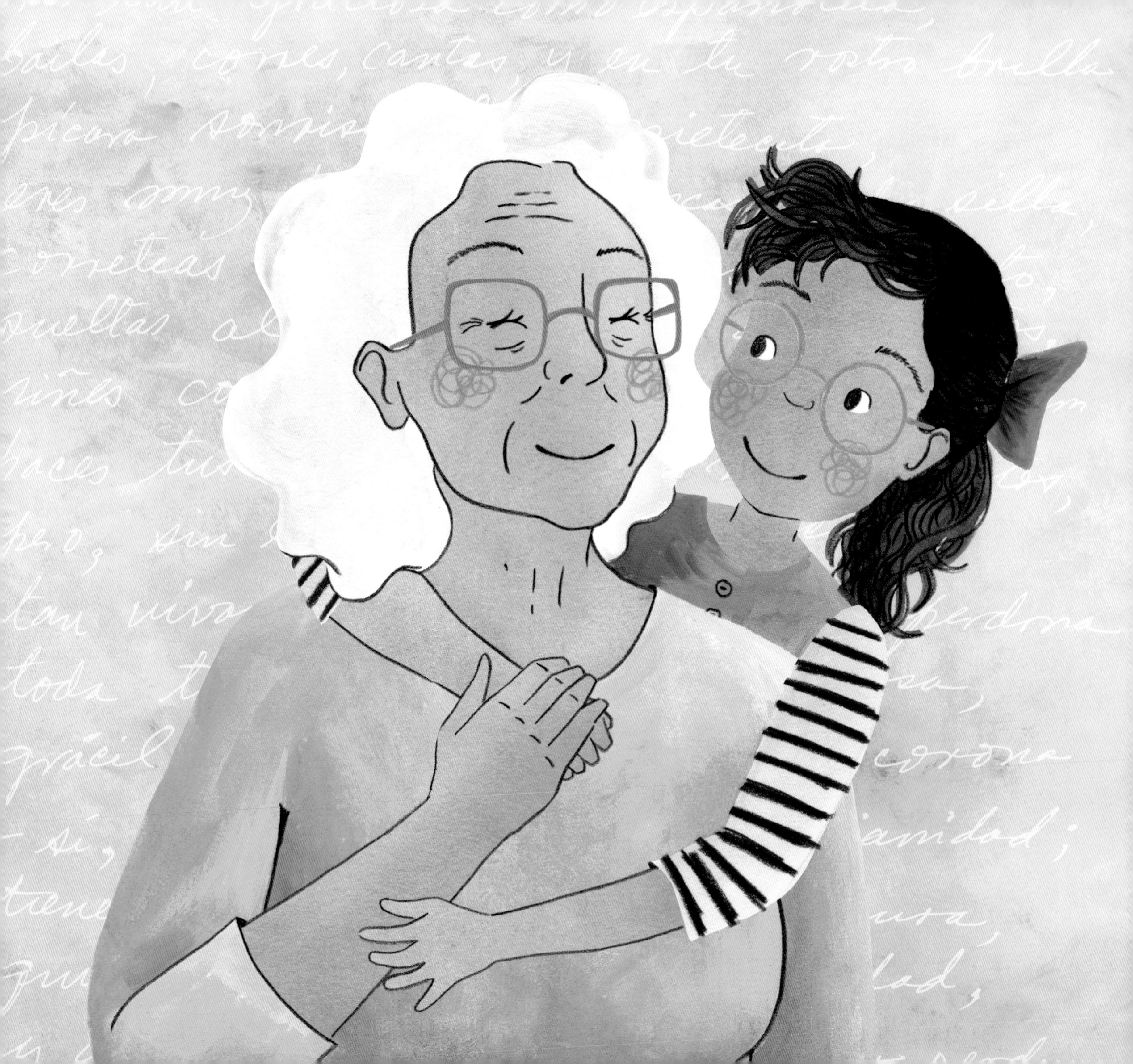
bailes, corres, cantas, y en tu rostro brilla

She was absolutely magical.

To Mom and Grandma, and
their enchanting hearts

First edition 2022

Library of Congress Catalog Card Number pending
ISBN 978-1-5362-0194-9 (English hardcover)
ISBN 978-1-5362-2256-2 (Spanish hardcover)

22 23 24 25 26 27 APS
1 2 3 4 5 6 7 8 9 10

Printed in Humen, Dongguan, China

This book was typeset in Youbee.
The illustrations were done in watercolor, gouache,
colored pencil, and digital collage.

Candlewick Press
99 Dover Street
Somerville, Massachusetts 02144

www.candlewick.com